The Box

Story and Illustrations by Mark Smith

It was a sunny summer's morning and all around
the garden the animals were waking up.

Sammy Sparrow stretched
her wings and chirped a happy tune to
welcome in the new day.

Henry Hedgehog tucked into a big breakfast of berries and grass roots.

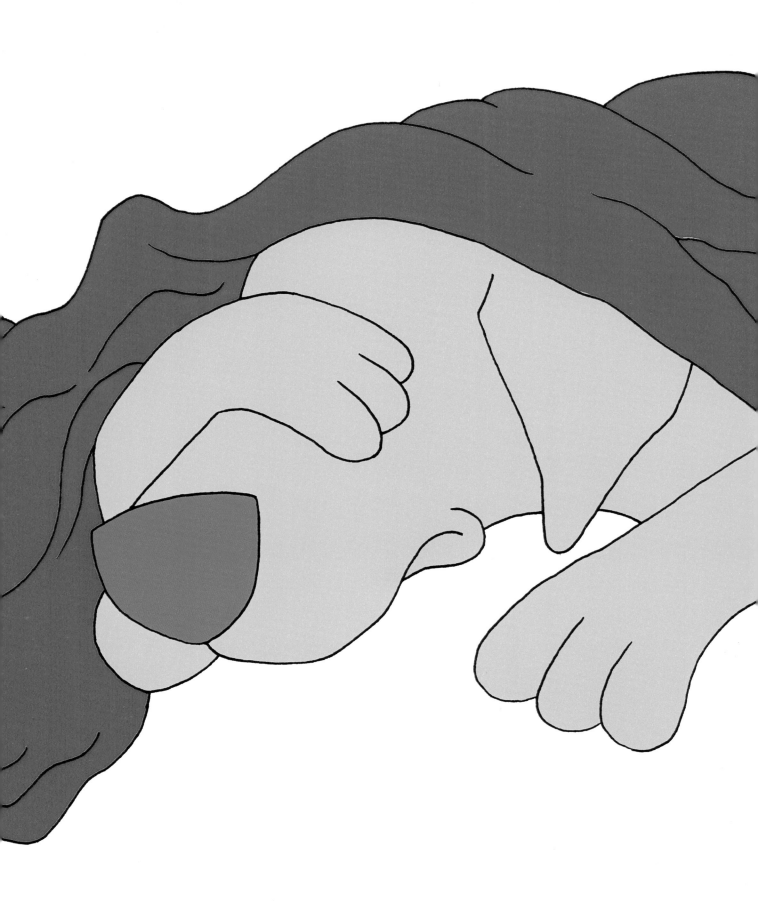

Declan Dog rolled over and
tried to go back to sleep.

And Maxwell Mouse bounced out of bed and did his exercises.

Once he had finished his exercises, Maxwell trotted happily along the tunnel that led out of his burrow and into the garden, but what he found there gave him an awful fright...

'Help!' Maxwell cried.
'Somebody, anybody,
come quickly!'
And everyone did come quickly.
Sammy sped down from her tree.
Henry hurried out from the bushes. Even dozy
Declan dashed out of his kennel.

'What's the matter, Maxwell?'
asked Sammy.

'This had better be important,'
Henry said. 'I was in the middle of
my breakfast!'

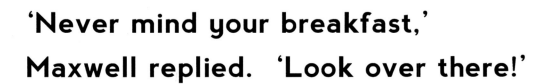

'Never mind your breakfast,'
Maxwell replied. 'Look over there!'

'What is it?' Declan asked.
Maxwell trembled as he answered.
'It's... THE BOX!'

'The Box is a terrible machine used to trap naughty animals,' Maxwell explained.

'Are you sure you're not thinking of a mouse trap?' Henry said.

'Oh no,' Maxwell replied. 'This is much, much worse!'

'Nonsense,' said Sammy. 'There's no such thing!'

'Maybe it's full of food,' Henry suggested. 'Cakes and buns, sandwiches and sweeties, all sorts of delicious treats...'

'I don't think anyone would put a big box of food in our garden,' Sammy interrupted, 'not with you around to gobble it all up!'

Declan started wagging his tail.
'Maybe there's a dog inside The Box,'
he said excitedly.

'I don't think a dog
would fit in there,
Declan,' Sammy said.

'Maybe it's a little dog,'
Declan continued.
'A puppy!'

'Well, there's only
one way to find out,'
Sammy declared,
marching towards The Box.

'Sammy, no!' Maxwell cried.

'What if it's a trap?'

'Or a dog?' Declan said. 'I hope
it's a dog!'

When Sammy reached The Box she unhooked the silver latch and swung the door open to find...

...a rabbit!

'Hello,' said the rabbit, 'my name's Ruby.
What's your name?'

Sammy and the other animals introduced themselves and showed Ruby Rabbit around the garden. They soon got used to having The Box nearby and were very pleased to have a nice new neighbour!

Super Speedster

There once was a man
Who could fly like a plane
And run really fast
Like a runaway train.

He flew over mountains
And ran over lakes,
But one problem he had
Was he didn't have brakes!

He ran all day long
And all through the night,
Or flew in the clouds,
Up there, out of sight.

But stopping was something
He just couldn't do,
No matter how hungry
Or tired he grew.

He ran in his sleep
And ate on the go.
But no matter what
His pace wouldn't slow.

Doctors and medics
From all over town
Searched for solutions
To make him slow down.

They tried different herbs
And spices galore,
But their clever concoctions
Just made him run more!

Then one fateful day,
As he soared across the sky,
Our hero suddenly realised
He'd forgotten how to fly!

Towards the ground he plummeted
And he landed with a thump.
Then upon his battered head
There grew a painful lump.

It wasn't till much later
When his pain had all but past
The super speedster noticed
He wasn't moving very fast.

He staggered to a wise man
Who told him very clear,
'Your flying days are over, son,
But don't you shed a tear.'

'For walking's very simple
And it really is quite fun,
Plus cycling's much quicker
If you've forgotten how to run.'

First thing's first,' our hero said,
'Before I make that leap,
I think that I'll be going home
For a long and peaceful sleep!'

Look out for

The Back Garden Gang's

next adventure...

Declan's Big Day